OLIVIA
helps with Christmas

by Ian Falconer

Atheneum Books for Young Readers
New York   London   Toronto   Sydney

'Twas the day before Christmas. Olivia and her family had been out

all morning, busy with last-minute shopping.

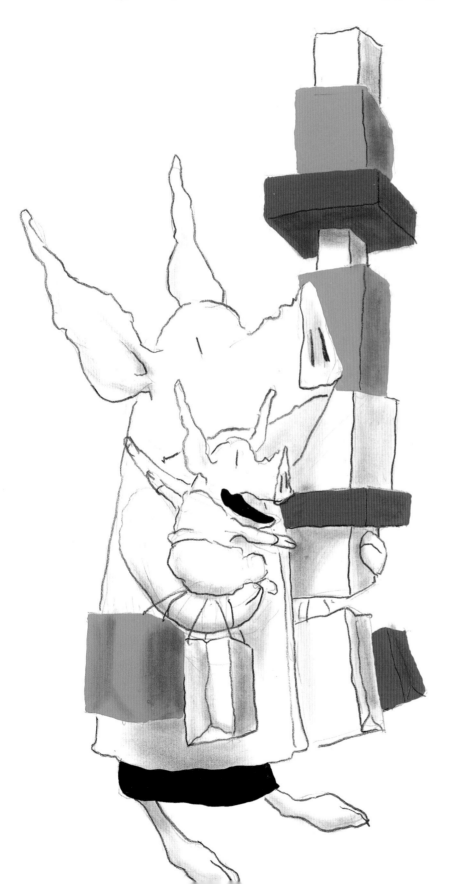

Olivia was exhausted,
yet there was still so
much to do.

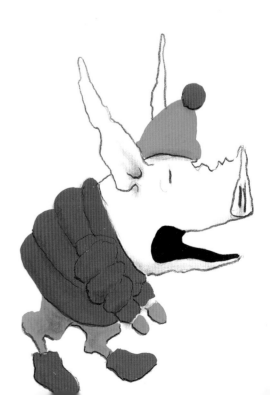

Olivia told her father and Ian to put up the tree,

so she could help her mother with William's lunch.

"Olivia, what are you feeding him?"

"Blueberry pie."

"Oh, darling, that's going to make him . . .

. . . sick!"

"Whoops."

By four o'clock Olivia was getting impatient.

"Sweetheart, Santa won't be here for hours,"
said her mother. "Now, wipe that soot off your
snout and help me untangle these lights."

"MOMMY!"

"Darling, it's much easier if you plug
them in first. There, isn't that better?"

Finally the tree was trimmed.

. . . . . . 5:00 PM . . . . . SANTA WATCH . . . . . NO SANTA . . . . . RAIN . . .

. . . tree?"

Olivia wanted to be even
more of a help. "Mommy,
may I set the table for
Christmas Eve dinner?"

"Oh yes, Olivia, that would
be very helpful."

"Why, that's beautiful, darling. Where
did you ever find that perfect little . . .

"Would you like to help me build a fire, Olivia?"

"DADDY! WHAT COULD YOU BE THINKING? DO YOU WANT TO COOK SANTA?!"

. 7:00 PM . . . . SANTA WATCH . . . . NO SANTA . . . . (BUT NO RAIN) . . .

After dinner the family gathered to sing carols.
Softly they started: "Angels we have heard on high,
sweetly singing o'er the plains."

Olivia always lets go for the chorus.

Glo-oooooo-O-ri-a!

Finally the most important task of the
night: leaving treats for Santa Claus.

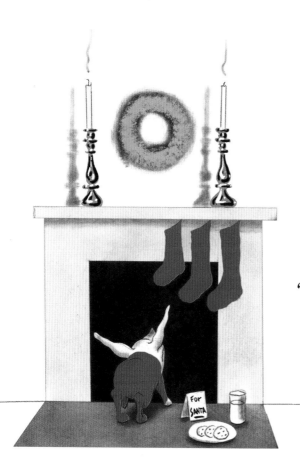

Olivia said, "Now it's time to wait." Her mother said, "Now it's time for bed."

But Olivia wasn't at all sleepy.

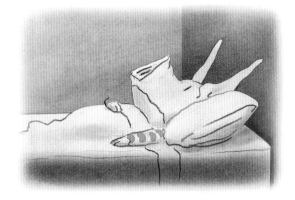

She tossed . . .

and she turned.

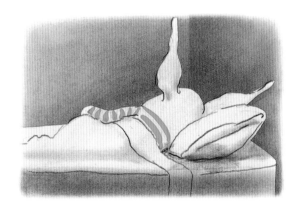

First she was hot.

Then she was cold.

Then she heard something on the roof.

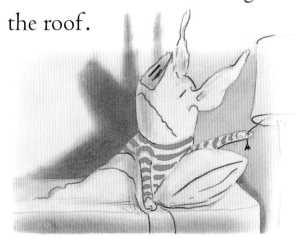

Could it be Santa???

It seemed she would never get to sleep—
until she woke up and saw it was morning.
Olivia ran to get her brothers.

Noiselessly they crept down the stairs.

SNOW!

PRESENTS!

STOCKINGS!

"And look!" cried Olivia.
"Santa ate all the cookies
and milk!"

"Now, children," said Olivia's mother. "Finish your breakfast, and then you can open your presents under the . . .

Some of Santa's offerings were better than others.

Pajamas.

Skis!

Sweater.

Sled!

Booties.

Maracas!

. . . tree."

"It looks like someone just learned to walk."

The children thanked their parents for a
wonderful Christmas and Olivia announced,
"Now I have a present for *you.*"

"It's a self-portrait. Won't it be beautiful over the fireplace?"

"Well," said Olivia, "I think I'll hit the slopes."

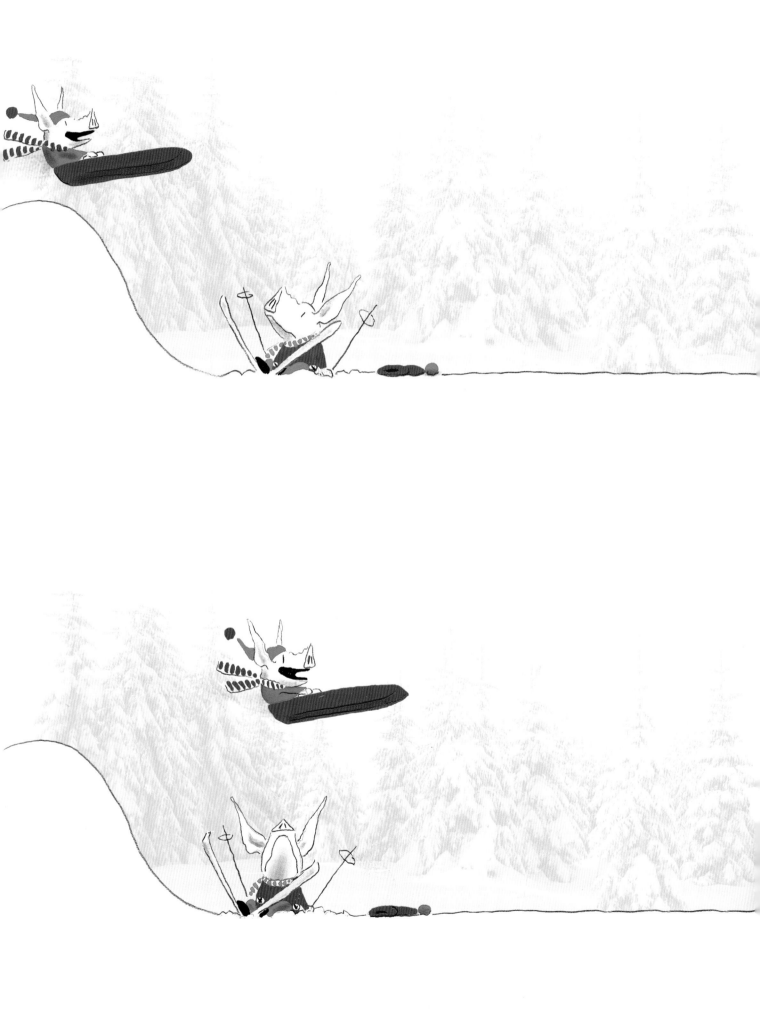

"Skiing takes more practice."

Olivia and Ian worked all afternoon to make a snowman.

Olivia dressed it.

That evening Olivia finally allowed her father to build a fire. The family sat and warmed their trotters while Olivia's mother brought them steaming mugs of hot soup.

Soon it was time for bed, but Olivia wasn't at all sleepy.

Or so she said. But before the lights were even out,
she fell into a deep, dreamless slumber . . .

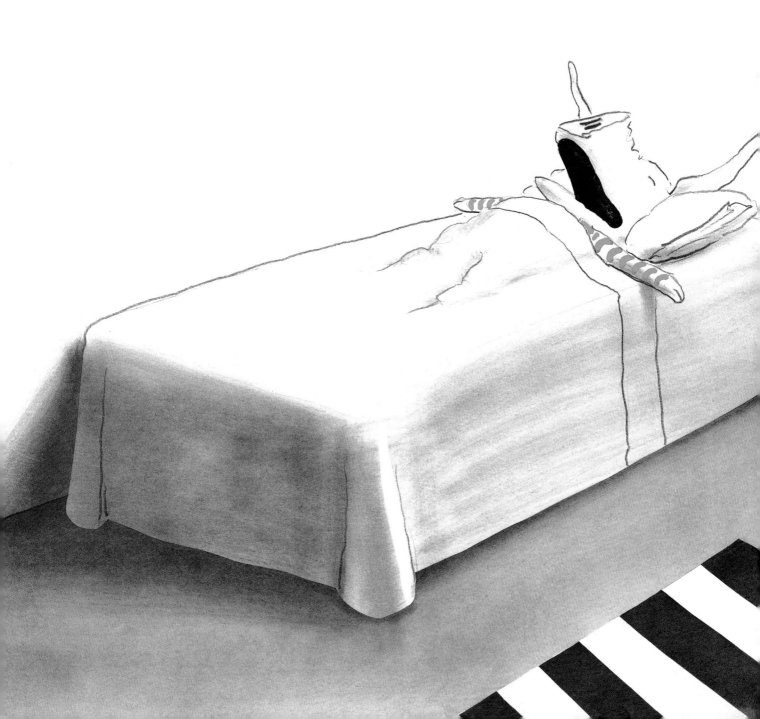

Well, not quite dreamless.